Dear Parent:

Psst . . . you're looking at the Super Secret Weapon of Reading. It's called comics.

STEP INTO READING® COMIC READERS are a perfect step in learning to read. They provide visual cues to the meaning of words and helpfully break out short pieces of dialogue into speech balloons.

Here are some terms commonly associated with comics:
  PANEL: A section of a comic with a box drawn around it.
  CAPTION: Narration that helps set the scene.
  SPEECH BALLOON: A bubble containing dialogue.
  GUTTER: The space between panels.

Tips for reading comics with your child:

• Have your child read the speech balloons while you read the captions.
• Ask your child: What is a character feeling? How can you tell?
• Have your child draw a comic showing what happens after the book is finished.

STEP INTO READING® COMIC READERS are designed to engage and to provide an empowering reading experience. They are also fun. The best-kept secret of comics is that they create lifelong readers. *And that will make you the real hero of the story!*

Jennifer L. Holm and Matthew Holm
Co-creators of the Babymouse and Squish series

To Tony, my very own rescue hero.
Lots of love forever.
xxx
—D.W.

Visit us on the Web!
StepIntoReading.com
randomhouse.com/kids

Educators and librarians, for a variety of teaching tools, visit us at RHTeachersLibrarians.com

Library of Congress Cataloging-in-Publication Data
Wojtowycz, David, author, illustrator.
Elephant Joe, brave firefighter! / by David Wojtowycz.
  pages cm. — (Step into reading. Step 2 comic reader)
Summary: At summer camp, Elephant Joe and Zebra Pete become firefighters
to rescue Dragon from a tree and put out a birthday cake fire.
ISBN 978-0-385-37406-4 (trade pbk.) — ISBN 978-0-375-97203-4 (lib. bdg.) —
ISBN 978-0-375-98196-8 (ebook)
[1. Firefighters—Fiction. 2. Birthdays—Fiction. 3. Rescue work—Fiction.
4. Camps—Fiction. 5. Elephants—Fiction. 6. Zebras—Fiction. 7. Dragons—Fiction.] I. Title.
PZ7.W81835Ej 2015 [E]—dc23 2014012170

Printed in the United States of America
10 9 8 7 6 5 4 3 2 1

This book has been officially leveled by using the F&P Text Level Gradient™ Leveling System.

ELEPHANT JOE,
Brave Firefighter!

by David Wojtowycz

Random House 🏠 New York

Dragon was so surprised, he flew up a tree!

19

Elephant Joe sucked up water with his trunk.

gulp
gulp

Hurry!

Elephant Joe spouted water all over the flames!

sploosh

Yay!
The fire is out!

Whew.